Andr

First published in Great Britain in 1991
by Simon & Schuster Young Books

Photoset in Rockwell by Goodfellow & Egan Ltd, Cambridge, England
Colour origination by Scantrans Pte Ltd, Singapore

Printed in Belgium by Proost International Book Production

Simon & Schuster Young Books
Simon & Schuster Ltd
Wolsey House
Wolsey Road
Hemel Hempstead HP2 4SS

BRITISH LIBRARY CATALOGUING IN PUBLICATION DATA
Sheldon, Dyan
Seymour finds a home.
1. English language. *Readers*
I. Title II. McMullen, Nigel
428.6

ISBN 0-7500-0591-2
ISBN 0-7500-0592-0 Pbk

Dyan Sheldon

Seymour finds a home

Illustrated by Nigel McMullen

SIMON & SCHUSTER

LONDON • SYDNEY • NEW YORK • TOKYO • SINGAPORE • TORONTO

CHAPTER ONE

Once upon a time, in a land very far from here, there was a young dragon whose name was Seymour. In many ways, Seymour was a very average dragon. He was the average size for a young dragon – about the size of a small horse. He was the average colour for a young dragon – green and blue with purple feet and a yellow stomach. And he was the average shape for a young dragon – rather like a pear with small, pointy ears and a long, sharp tail.

Seymour had the average
number of toes, and scales,
and eyes and nostrils
for a young dragon, too.

In fact, if you had put all the young dragons of that very faraway land together in a long line, you would have said that they were all pretty much the same. You would have thought that once you'd seen one dragon you'd more or less seen them all. But you would have been wrong. Seymour was different.

Seymour could roar until the ground shook, just like all the other dragons.

Seymour could belch until his eyes popped, just like all the other dragons.

Seymour could run and play until the sun went down, just like all the other dragons.

And, just like all the other dragons, Seymour could frighten the bravest knight with a flick of his powerful tail.

There was one thing, however, that Seymour couldn't do. He couldn't breathe fire, like all the other dragons could. Not even a very small fire. Not even enough to light a match.

Seymour would huff and puff and growl and roar, but when he opened his mouth he didn't breathe one single spark. Seymour would roll his eyes, and stamp his foot, and thump his tail, but when he opened his mouth all that came out was snow.

Cold, white snow.

If the day was especially warm and sunny, he breathed rain. Clear, wet rain.

And sometimes, if he was in a very bad mood, he breathed tiny tornadoes.

But he never breathed fire and smoke.

Obviously, Seymour had problems.

For one thing, it was very difficult to make beautiful princesses scream by breathing snow showers. It made them chilly and grumpy, but it didn't actually scare them. Sometimes they even found it funny.

"Hahahahaha," they would laugh. "Get a load of the dragon with the snow."

For another thing, knights were not too keen on fighting a dragon who breathed sudden storms. It was damp and cold and it rusted their armour. And most of the time they couldn't fight because they were laughing so hard.

"Hehehehehe," they giggled. "You're not a dragon, you're a spring shower with ears."

But the worst thing of all was that none of the other young dragons wanted to play with Seymour. Not even once in a while. Not even when there was no one else to play with. Not even when they were bored and had nothing to do. Not ever. Not at all.

This wasn't because Seymour wasn't a nice dragon.

This wasn't because Seymour wasn't a friendly dragon.

This wasn't because he cheated at games or because he was a bully.

It was because every time one of the other dragons roared and breathed fire, Seymour roared and put it out. The other dragons didn't find this amusing.

"I can blow a flame that's red, yellow and blue," boasted one young dragon. "It can reach the tops of the trees."

"I can blow a flame that's as wide as a river and as hot as the sun," bragged another.

"And I can melt a mountain with my breath," announced a third.

"But Seymour," they all shouted together, "Seymour can only water the grass."

And then they laughed and laughed and laughed. And went off to play by themselves.

CHAPTER TWO

Even Seymour's father was a little fed up with him.

"It's not that I don't love you just the way you are, son," said Seymour's father. "But it would be nice if you could breathe a fireball or two now and then." He shook some snow from his head. "All this bad weather is a little upsetting."

Seymour became very lonely and sad. He sat by himself at the entrance of his cave, watching the other young dragons playing in the fields.

They laughed. They roared. They rolled on their backs in the long grass and waved their feet in the air. They wiggled their ears. The other young dragons had a lot of fun.

But Seymour wasn't having fun. He wasn't having any fun at all. It was as though the sun shone over the other young dragons, but over Seymour there was only a small, black cloud. A small black cloud filled with snow.

"What use is a dragon who can only breathe bad weather?" Seymour asked himself.

"None at all," the other young dragons seemed to answer.

Seymour's mother took him to the doctor.

The doctor peered down Seymour's throat. "Say ahhhhh," said the doctor. "Ahhhhh," said Seymour.

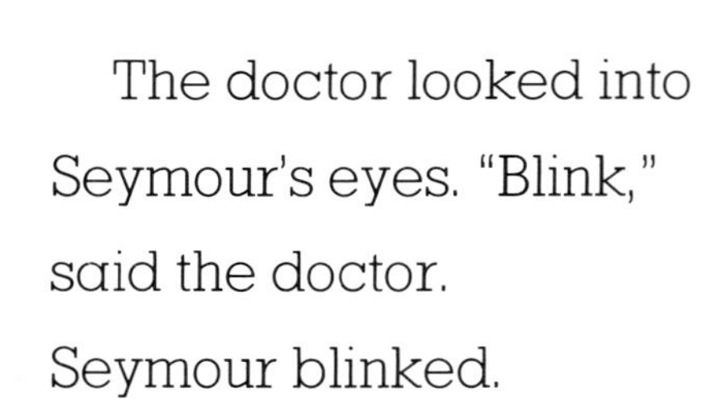

The doctor looked into Seymour's eyes. "Blink," said the doctor. Seymour blinked.

"Make terrible faces," commanded the doctor.

Seymour made himself look as terrible as he could.

The doctor examined Seymour's scales. "Gallop around the room," ordered the doctor.

Seymour galloped.

"Pretend I'm a beautiful young princess, up in a tower," said the doctor. "Show me what you would do."

Seymour closed his eyes very tight. He tried to imagine the doctor as a beautiful young princess, looking out of a castle window. He took a deep deep breath. He thought of all the things that dragons think of when they are about to burn a castle to the ground.

And then he roared.

He roared and roared with all his might.

The floor shook. The ceiling trembled.

Seymour's mother gasped. "Oh!"

The doctor yelped in surprise. "Eek!"

But when Seymour opened his eyes again there was no thick black smoke. There were no bright orange flames.

There were only his mother and the doctor. They were standing up to their knees in snow.

The doctor cleared his throat. "Well," he said gently, "perhaps you're just not thinking hard enough."

Seymour shook the snow from his back and sighed. "What use is a dragon who can only breathe blizzards?" he asked himself.

CHAPTER THREE

Seymour was tired of having no one to play with. He was tired of being teased all the time. He was fed up with feeling so useless. Seymour decided to go away. After all, he told himself, the world was filled with all sorts of different and marvellous places. Surely there was one that was just right for him.

Seymour kissed his parents goodbye. "There is somewhere in the world where I'll fit in," he told them bravely. "All I have to do is find it."

Seymour's mother hugged him. "Be a good dragon, love," she whispered. "Keep warm, and don't forget to eat your greens." She wiped a tear from her eye.

Seymour's father hugged him. "You be careful, son," said Seymour's father. He shook a few snowflakes from his shoulder. "We'll be thinking about you," he said.

"Don't worry about me," said Seymour. "I'm going to find the place where I belong."

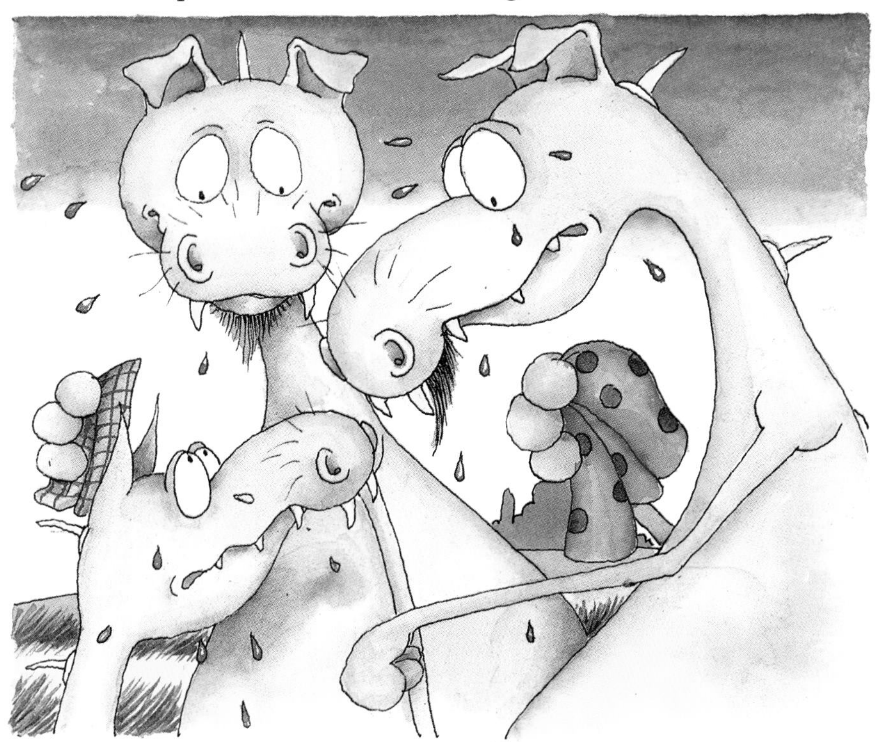

Seymour walked for days on end. He went deep into the forest, where dragons never went.

It wasn't long before Seymour discovered just why dragons never went there.

It was dark and damp in the forest. Dragons liked to stretch out on large rocks in the afternoon and nap in the sun. But there were no large rocks in the forest, only pine cones and dead leaves and broken

branches. The trees were so tall and so close together that there wasn't any sun.

It was crowded in the forest. Dragons liked to romp and frolic. But there were so many trees and animals in the forest that there was no room for a dragon to romp or frolic. There wasn't even any room in which a dragon could swing his long, spiky tail.

Most of the forest creatures slept in nests or burrows or dens. Dragons slept in caves. But every cave that Seymour found already had a bear in it.

"Get out of here!" growled the bears.

"Where am I going to sleep?" asked Seymour.

"Sleep in a tree, like we do," said the squirrels.

But Seymour couldn't find a hollow big enough.

"Sleep in a tree, like we do," said the birds.

But Seymour couldn't find the right sized nest.

"Why don't you sleep in a tree, like we do?" suggested the opossums.

But Seymour broke the branch.

"Maybe the forest isn't where I belong after all," said Seymour.

None of the other creatures disagreed.

CHAPTER FOUR

Seymour left the forest. He walked for days on end, until at last he came to a green, peaceful valley.

There was a large, busy farm in the valley. There were cows in the meadow. There were ducks and geese in the pond. There were pigs and chickens in the yard.

"This looks more like it," said Seymour. "There's plenty of sunshine here!" He flicked his tail happily. "There's lots of room!"

Seymour loped into the meadow, ready to play. "Yoo hoo!" he called. "Here I am!"

But the cows weren't very happy about having a dragon running through their meadow. He made the ground shake. He made the trees tremble. He made a lot of noise.

"Everything was very quiet until you came along," grumbled the cows. "Now we can't even hear ourselves chew."

"I only wanted to have some fun," said Seymour.

"You'll have to have fun somewhere else," said the cows.

Seymour went to have fun with the ducks and the geese. After all, he had always liked water.

"Hi there!" cried Seymour. "Can I swim too?"

But with Seymour in the pond there wasn't much room for the ducks and the geese.

"Get out! Get out!" quacked the ducks.

"Watch where you put that tail," honked the geese.

"I only wanted to play," said Seymour.

"Well, you'll have to play somewhere else," said the ducks and the geese. "You can't stay here with us."

Seymour slunk off to the barnyard.

But the barnyard wasn't as big as the meadow or as open as the pond. There were fences and coops and troughs in the way.

"Look out!" squealed the pigs. "You're too big to roll in the mud."

"Be careful!" warned the chickens. "You're knocking everything down!"

Seymour sat in the middle of the yard and tried to make himself as small as possible.

But the damage had already been done.

The farmer came running from the barn. "Look what you've done!" he shouted. "Look at this mess! Get out of here, you clumsy dragon. Get off my farm!"

"I'm going, I'm going," said Seymour. "I can tell when I'm not wanted."

CHAPTER FIVE

Seymour walked for days on end. The further he walked, the warmer and sunnier the weather became. At last he came to an enormous desert.

"There's certainly enough room here for a dragon," said Seymour. "And it could certainly do with a little rain." Seymour began to cheer up. Perhaps he had found his perfect place at last.

But Seymour didn't stay cheered up for long. He soon discovered that dragons weren't very good at

walking in sand. It got between their toes and stuck in their scales.

There were no shady glens or cosy caves in the desert either.

And the desert wasn't really the place for having a lot of fun.

"Life in the desert is hard," said the camels. "There's no time for games and nonsense here."

"That's right," said the sand cats. "Everyone in the desert has to work just to survive. You can't run about and play here."

Seymour thought that he might make friends by creating a storm.

But when he roared he blew the sand across the desert, and the tinier animals with it.

"Stop! Stop!" they all shouted together. "You're destroying our homes!"

And when he breathed a storm they shouted even more.

"No, no!" they screamed. "We can't have all this rain on the desert. You're mixing everything up!"

Seymour brushed some sand from his scales. "Do you want me to go?" he asked.

Silently, the desert animals pointed the way across the sand.

CHAPTER SIX

Seymour walked for days on end. He walked as far from the forest, and the farm, and the desert as he could get. He walked until he came to a land that was completely frozen and perfectly white. As far as he could see there was absolutely nothing there. It was definitely big enough for a young dragon. He could breathe blizzards here and no one would notice. He could make a storm and no one would care.

"This must be it," Seymour said to himself. "This must be my place."

The other animals were very friendly.

"Have a raw fish," offered the polar bears.

But dragons weren't very fond of raw fish. Seymour's nostrils quivered. He made a face. "Yuk," said Seymour. "This smells like old boots."

"Come in for a swim then," called the seals.

But dragons weren't really suited to swimming in icy pools. Seymour's teeth began to chatter. His scales began to freeze. Icicles dripped from his chin. "I-i-is it always this cold?" stammered Seymour.

The foxes were chasing each other through the snow. "Oh, no," they laughed. "It's often much colder than this."

Never before had Seymour wished that he could breathe fire as much as he wished that he could breathe fire now. Even his eyelashes ached from the cold. He snapped an icicle from his chin. "Perhaps this isn't the place for me after all," Seymour sighed.

CHAPTER SEVEN

Seymour walked for days on end. Then one sunny morning, just as he was wondering if he would ever find a place to call home, he saw spirals of dark grey smoke in the distance. Seymour stopped. He sniffed the air. He could smell grass burning. He listened. He could hear cries for help.

Without a second thought, Seymour started galloping over the hill. He raced down the road until he came to a burning field. In front of him was a wall of flames. It looked to Seymour as though the whole world were on fire. Behind the wall of flames he heard crying and shouting.

Seymour closed his eyes. He took a deep deep breath. Then, with a terrible roar, he breathed a storm of rain and snow. He breathed a storm that shook the mountains and bent the trees. He roared again and again, until he had put out every bit of fire with his wet and icy breath.

When the smoke cleared, Seymour looked around.

There were his mother and father. There were all the other dragons. They all looked very happy to see him.

"Seymour!" cried his mother. She ran over and gave him a big kiss. "Seymour! I knew you'd come home!"

"And not a second too soon, either," said Seymour's father. He gave him a big kiss, too. "If you hadn't turned up when you did, we would all have lost our homes."

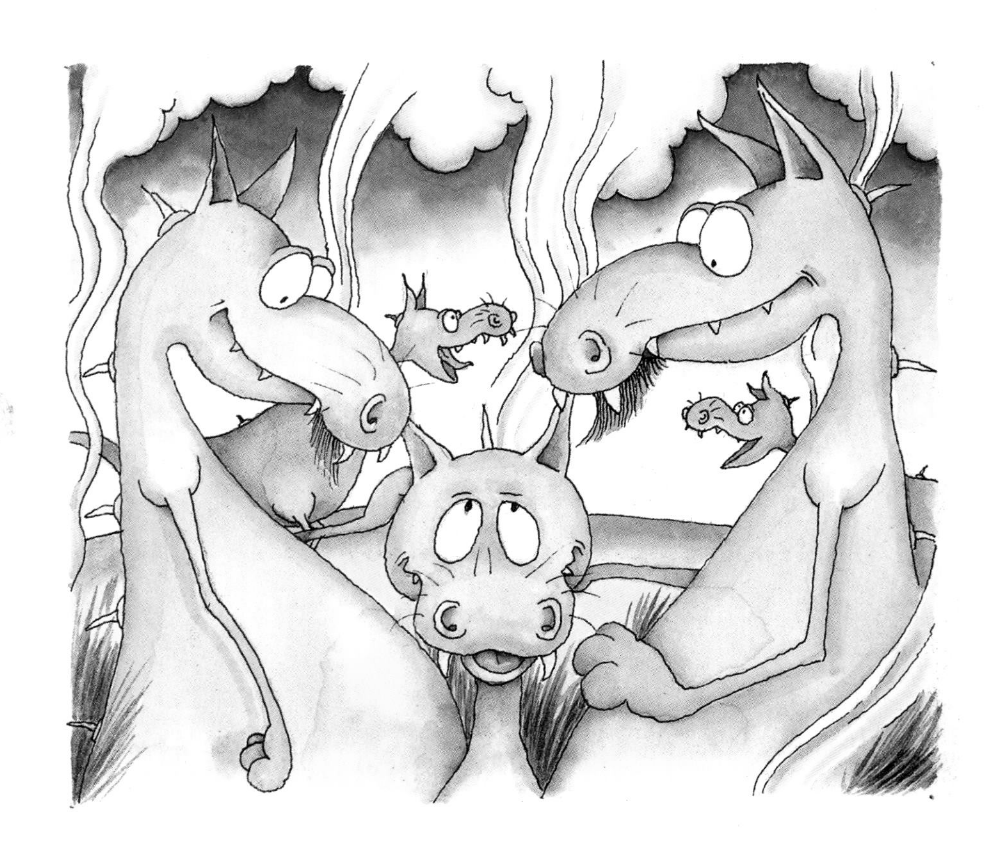

The other dragons were jumping up and down with excitement. "Seymour!" they shouted. "Seymour you're a hero!"

Seymour cuddled between his parents.

Seymour's father shook snow from his head. "It's good to have you home, son," said Seymour's father.

"And it's very good to be home," smiled Seymour.

PRINTED IN BELGIUM BY
proost
INTERNATIONAL BOOK PRODUCTION